The Pied Piper of Hamelin

This edition first published in 2007 by
Sea-to-Sea Publications
1980 Lookout Drive
North Mankato
Minnesota 56003

Printed in China

Library of Congress Cataloging-in-Publication Data
Adeney, Anne.
  The Pied Piper of Hamelin / by Anne Adeney.
   p. cm. -- (First fairy tales)
  Summary: A simplified version of the tale in which the Pied Piper pipes the village free
of rats but, when the villagers refuse to pay him for his services, he exacts a terrible revenge.
  ISBN-13: 978-1-59771-072-5
   1. Pied Piper of Hamelin (Legendary character)- -Legends. [1. Pied Piper of Hamelin
(Legendary character)- -Legends. 2. Folklore- -Germany- -Hamelin.] I. Pied Piper of
Hamelin. English. II. Title. III. Series.

PZ8.A226Pi 2006
398.2--dc22
[E]

2005057544

9 8 7 6 5 4 3 2

Published by arrangement with the Watts Publishing Group Ltd, London

Series Editor: Jackie Hamley
Series Advisor: Linda Gambrell, Dr. Barrie Wade
Series Designer: Peter Scoulding

The **Pied Piper** of **Hamelin**

Retold by Anne Adeney

Illustrated by Jan Lewis

SEA-TO-SEA
Mankato Collingwood London

Once upon a time, there
was a town called Hamelin.

Hamelin was a fine town,
but it had a big
problem.

7

Rats! There were rats everywhere!

Rats bit the babies.

They ate up every scrap
of food.

Something had to be
done. A strange man
came to Hamelin.

"I am the Pied Piper,"
said the strange man.

"I can get rid of all
your rats."

"First you must promise to pay me," the Pied Piper said.

gnats ~ 1 bag of gold
mice ~ 2 bags of gold
rats ~ 3 bags of gold
vampire bats ~ 4 bags of gold
snakes ~ 5 bags of gold
Dragons ~ 10 bags of gold

The people promised to
pay the Pied Piper three
bags of gold.

The Pied Piper began
to play his pipe.

His magic music made all the rats follow him.

They danced to his tune
down to the river.

The rats were never seen in Hamelin again. The people were so happy!

But they did not pay the
gold as they had promised.

The Pied Piper was

very angry.

He began to play his
pipe again.

This time, his magic music
made all the children
follow him.

They danced to his tune
up to the mountains and
into a wonderful kingdom.
Only one boy could
not keep up.

The children were never
seen again. After that,
the sad people of
Hamelin always
kept their promises.

If you have enjoyed this First Fairy Tale, why not try another one? There are six books in the series:

978-1-59771-071-8

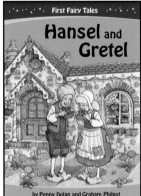

978-1-59771-075-6

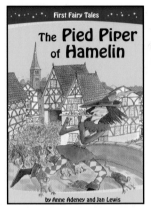

978-1-59771-072-5

978-1-59771-076-3

978-1-59771-073-2

978-1-59771-074-9